AF123072

The legend of the Blood Biters

Ross Anthony Chandler

I hear the panting getting louder the closer it gets the more I feel it toys with me all of a sudden a howl that makes even the branches on the trees shiver all of a sudden it hits me this is the beginning of the end…..

The blood biters
By
Ross Chandler

chapter 1: THE BEGINING

I herd loud panting getting closer and closer all that is running through my head is this the end of me I keep running thinking I stand a chance against this beast as I was about to scream for help it hit me this was the begging of the end

2 days before

I was out with my best friend their was supposed to be about fifteen of us but only ten decided to turn up we decided to go camping as it was my 18th birthday. I was hopeful my mum would give me some beer or something but she gave me a hug and told me to be on my way to college but she didn't no where I was going tonight and that would make me a man. We are being dared to go camp in the forbidden Forrest obviously there is a girl involved the most beautiful girl iv ever met but anyway my name is Anthony my best friends are coming with me and so are the other ten my best friends are called john Epson and Eddie shark our parents when we where younger called us the three musketeers me and Eddie are still best friends but johns more an outsider because we kinda became more popular than him. Anyway we are all looking at the Forrest remembering the story as to why its forbidden everyone has their own view but the main problem is that every month a company of soldiers disappear some people say that wolves own it and that a pack of wild wolves kills them but a lot of the elderly say that its half men half wolves my they is that the government is working on something important I mean people used to walk through the Forrest a hundred years ago with no problems now its a dark place and all we are told is for our own stay to stay away from the Forrest I think its bullshit besides this girl I like is fit shes called Becky we all look at the Forrest and say tomorrow we will venture deep inside the Forrest and we will see this evil yer right anyway I wanna impress this girl so I will do whatever I can to make her want to be my girlfriend so tomorrow hear I come to become the man I want to be

Chapter 2: THE FORREST AWAITS

today Is the day I go to the Forrest I feel fear among all of the girls and the guys that are with us but im not scared of anything so I make sure everything is ready to go Eddie and john are ready last night a group of soldiers disappeared again but that is the normal thing around hear a couple of people have backed out but Becky is still coming with us im so proud before we set off I said to her will you go out with me and she replied of course she would anyway we are just waiting for it to be dark enough to slip past the soldiers and the imperial guard put their to stop anyone passing through into the darkest Forrest all ten of us run through their defense and head deep into the Forrest we start to run in case we where spotted how much I wish to this day we had turned back when we had the chance we hear the howl of a wolf but figure its nothing as we hear it every month at this time of the moon phase however it does send shivers through our bones last month a company of soldiers disappeared from the area and a few weeks later we found parts of bone and flesh we where told it was a training exercise I think the government is covering their tracks i mean id rather believe that the government is working on something secret than the idea of what some people believe such as vampires demons and ghosts hahaha I laugh in the face of them people they are just crazy I looked at Becky and thought full moon this is my chance to get the most romantic form of kiss a man can get she looks at me with her beautiful blue eyes and blond hair I lean in and kiss her so gently then the three musketeers must set up their tents but I put hers up first so that I could make a good impression and we have all set up camp but iv made two of the lads keep watch in case any soldiers should accidentally stumble into us and arrest us or worse kill us I laid on the grass for a few moments and looked up into the nights sky to stare at the full moon with Becky in my arms I felt weird though because out of the corner of my eyes I saw something on the edge of the camp I looked out and couldn't see anything it must be my eyes playing tricks on me all of a sudden their was a howl I thought Jamie you idiot and ran to where he was because he was on watch we carried on as normal I went into mine and Becky's tent and turned on the radio we all listen and hear that the army had had yet another training accident and that nobody had survived and then the shocking news came through our names where read out among the missing people our parents must have reported us to the police they had searched the town and nothing of us no one had seen us all day they are hoping we can hear them and that if we are in the Forrest to make some kind of fire to show we are alive all of a sudden I hear a scream one of the girls was crying and screaming running into the camp with red on her hands it was Jamie's girlfriend running to the center of the camp I try to calm her down and talk to her ask her what she saw she replied "Jamie he's he's dead I just went to see if he was OK and if he wanted some company and he just collapsed in front of me" I then told the boys to stay with the girls while I go check it out I walk over to what was once my friend and see he's been torn to pieces the thing is we didn't even see it whatever it was the girl that ran to us with the blood says lets get out of hear I scream at her no we cannot go now if we leave this area we would be like lambs to the slaughter if we wait till morning we have the advantage of being able to see in the day time they all nod and agree to keep within shouting distance

2 hours later 11:00 p.m

Two more of the group have disappeared we no we are not alone hear we just can't seem to keep up with these monsters or people ether way me and the lads have started to make a barricade so that if anything tires to take us we will see it coming over the last two hours iv become a solider just waiting and preying we have signaled so that they no we are alive and have the radio on we hear on the radio that the imperial guard and the elite fighters are going to come in and get us out everyone is scared even I am I mean I no I said I'm not scared of things but I'm terrified I just want to make it home no one is talking just all sitting together Becky is trying to calm them all down but its just not working I all of a sudden break down and say this is all my fault I brought u all out hear iv lost all of the missing and Jamie I will never forget them and will hate my self for it Becky comes to me and comforts me and says no we all came out hear to see if the stories where true and turns out yes they are but don't blame your self for this stuff all we need to do is stick together you are our leader Anthony even though its not ideal being hear we are hear and there is nothing we can do we hear a transition from the army they are sending in a contingency force voluntary veterans are coming and the imperial force that involves 16 specialists so we are relived

11:59 p.m

Only 9 soldiers arrived and the imperial army was already with us they look terrified a few of them are wounded I ask if they need anything and they instantly respond to me with stupid children going against the rules of the government we came to get you so that maybe you would learn your lesson is this all of you I check yes he said we've got 10 missing kids and Ur saying here is only 6 of you left where are the rest I said one is dead the other 3 missing the commander then said their blood is on your hands the missing yes they are dead we will have to hold up hear for a while how are your supplies I said we have food and water he said right kids now you are all about to become adults each of you take a gun and aim at the tree line and watch for any movement while my men set up our camp we will remain hear till first light then we move out we hear howls and I just shout stupid wolves leave us alone the commander pulls a knife to my through and says if you give our position away more than you already have I will kill you and say that the werewolves got you I laugh and say werewolves he says fine laugh all you want you will see soon enough how do u think I lost so many good men because of you pathetic children ran away to see the Forrest

1:00 a.m

A few soldiers have died and a few of us so called kids have died but im still alive for now at least the guy who was in charge had a blood lust after half his men where killed he ran out and told them to kill him they did exactly that so he died in front of us at first we thought their was only one it turns out its an entire pack I all of a sudden have the urge to run im sick of waiting hear to die so I run out into the Forrest I drop the gun its to heavy the new found leader tried to stop me I just side step him and run into the Forrest into the pitch black running deeper and deeper I herd gunfire from the camp id left I felt sorrow but there is no way I could turn back now I was to far away from them and I thought I was close to the edge of the Forrest

chapter 3: THE BITE

I had been running away for about two hours I realized id been running in circles I could hear screams and gunfire but I couldn't go back for them now if I was to make it out of hear I would tell my story of what happened how they valiantly gave their lives for us all of a sudden silence feel it was devastating because while their was noise I didn't feel alone now silence and I couldn't bare it I felt closer to the edge I could see one of the houses I herd loud panting getting closer and closer all that is running through my head is this the end of me I keep running thinking I stand a chance against this beast as I was about to scream for help it hit me it hit me to the floor pinned me down I looked up at this vial creature and thought goodbye world it plunged its teeth into my neck and started to drain me but then it pulled away and left me to drift into an unconscious state I was falling into darkness so deep...

Chapter 4: SECOND LIFE

when I awoke I felt some what stronger my wound had healed I herd noise around me I sit up I was in a cave some where I have no idea but I can smell blood I hear a howl really close by I turn around and see a pool of water I look into it and stare into the eyes of a monster I realize with horror iv become one of them I can see my self howling towards the moon but I cant control myself I try to scream out to people but every-time that I did I just growled even though I was a monster I felt amazing aside the fact id become what I feared but why did that thing leave me for death or did it know id become one of them who knows I can smell food now and im ohhh so hungry it feels like a lifetime since iv eaten so I start to run and within seconds I was back at what was our camp it felt like I was faster I saw a couple of the other creatures feasting on the human bodies the thing is I wasn't even disturbed by it if anything I was enjoying it that might seem wrong to you but I wasn't human anymore so the rules must be different anyway one of the other creatures held up a body it was johns I felt nothing no sadness no pain or anger I took the body off it and started to drain it of blood I felt so much more powerful I could hear a girls cry I knew who it was but I left it for last when I finally turned round the corner I found Becky my last human girlfriend I decided to leave her to live and go back to the humans I picked her up with one hand and ran her to where I fell I put her down and let her run off to her house she was crying all the way but she thought I was dead so their was no problem everything would sort itself out now she was safe at least I returned to the feast but looked back at her she could tell it was me and screamed at me to stop the change the moon was way to powerful to change back now I roared at her she cried and ran away then the army turned up so I disappeared I didn't want to be their next experiment iv herd of their methods I think im a wolf and a man so im a werewolf even though I didn't believe it I had the evidence that proved I was I felt so guilty for all the people that had died over the years and yet I also realized that their sacrifice has not gone to waste anyway I ran back to the other wolves I felt like I could talk to them lie we all understood each other it was weird how I could understand their growls saying welcome Anthony to the pack

Chapter 5: LEARNING THE ROPES

apparently as a wolf I must learn to control myself in front of the elders I found this out after we had finished feasting on the humans remains the wolves all said we need to return home before the sunrises otherwise we will be lost and so they all turned and ran and I ran too I figured if anyone was to know what was going on it would be them within seconds we reached a old fortress I had heard legends about this place that only wolves where aloud hear and true to their words pure wolves where hear they bowed to us as we passed through the gates as if we where parading even though I have never been hear before it was like a celebration I was welcomed by all the other werewolves it felt like for the first time I was wanted until I met Grey hound who hates new blood he stood infrequent of me and said the elders want to inspect you to see if you match our criteria if not you will be destroyed I swear I herd him say I pray they destroy you I shrugged I was supposed to be dead anyway I walked into their tent they had silver swords I felt weak and turned back into my human form the elders and leaders of the pack looked at me and said you must be the chosen one because no one can block this they throw a silver sword at me it cuts but heals fast they then say the prophecy is becoming true alert the tribe our leader has arrived but first he must find his feet are you willing to train for a few weeks and be tested I said yes sure I will all knowing and all powerful leaders I bow to them and ask if I can do anything for them they bow to me witch was really weird firstly im praised by people then im bowed to by the leaders and told im a prophecy I hope its a good one seriously doubt that though as soon as I left the tent I was strait away thrown into combat training and into running by the end of the first few days I was exhausted as where all the other trainees some even died because they where to dangerous the nights where long and the training hard but those of us who stood became a pack and where aloud into the wild the first place I wanted to go was to the camp to collect some of my old equipment but apparently wolves are not aloud to wield guns as soon as I touched it I was burning so I let go its in law that we are only ever allowed to wield a sword and the swords are from the fortress supposedly a chosen one cant even wield a sword I must learn to use my hands for combat and that sucks so bad at the moment im only ever able to use a sword if the fortress gets attacked and that hasn't happened apparently in two thousand years so no need to worry

Chapter 6: DEATH MOUNTIN

after we had all been trained and settled into the fort I asked the elders if I could take a look at the surroundings of the Forrest they responded only go with an experienced wolf so that you can always find Ur way home and so I dragged one of the other newbies with me even though im a newbie too and then guess who els comes along with us Grey hound he wants to test me see if I am truly their Savior or their destroyer anyway it took us 3 days of walking running and wolf form to get to the mountains bottom I have made a few friends a female wolf that when she is in human form is absolutely stunning her name is Elisa I think she likes me but I am unsure if she feels the same who knows many we are destiny maby beauty really was the beast before she turned I wonder how long shes been with the wolves before I can ask her she answers my question she was only new blood like me I smiled and said well then I guess we can get closer we need to stick together she looked at me and smiled then replied id like that Grey hound was tired so he told us we shall rest hear for the night me and Elisa huddled together even though it wasn't against the rules all the others seemed to keep away from her I was so protective of her it was unreal she looked at me before I close my eyes and kissed me on the nose I thought that was a bit weird we had only met literally half a day before it felt so good but so quick I was worried I be played and with these new emotion god knows how it would effect me but for now it feels amazing and that's all that counted I then fell asleep I awoke to the sounds of scrams coming from the top of the mountain Grey hound was way ahead of us and ran towards the screams he changed to wolf as id we so we could move faster I said to Elise stay close to me and we ran together in sync with each others movements when we got to the top all we could see is flames and utter carnage Grey hound had a old man in his arms and he was bleeding so badly it was hard for us not to want to kill him but we needed to no what had happened he said in his final breath you cannot run you can not escape the demons have arrived no one will be saved then died with that a raw like thunder hit the floor it shook more than an earth quake and yet I still felt no fear as if it was all just natural to me but we no we are gonna have to fight so everybody draws their sword mine is taken from me because im the chosen one I am supposed to lead us to victory this battle will be glorious Grey says to us all and to watch him but all of a sudden we realize why the place was on fire something was crawling out of the ground

Grey hound instantly new what this thing was and told us to run away and try to find some form of cover so we ran into a cave and asked what it was he then looked at us and said who is ready to die for the entire of this planet I stood judging by I am the chosen one he said I thought so just what he wanted he pushes me away from the rest and says I am not going to lie what we are up against I my self made sure that could never return it appears this area is now in control not by the magic of the druids but by the demonic powers of hell we need to alert the council and with that something grabbed his leg from outside I could see him smile and say I will see you on the other side brother and with that I herd him fighting whatever these demons where he put up one hell of a fight by the sounds of it but eventually we heard him scream then silence I told everyone to remain slant while I check round the area their was literally his body and about 14 corpses of whatever they where he did fight hard and well I tell the others to help me carry him and the bodies of what ever they are back to the fortress's when we finally arrived a couple of days later the elders asked to speak to them strait away talk was spreading that we where under attack but from what and the elders wanted to see the bodies of those Grey hound had killed when they see their faces turn to the paintings behind them that are of the prophecy I look at the paintings and realize with horror it is me in the picture carrying the body of a fallen warrior with demonic following me I realized what this men it men that no matter what now destiny would make everything for me near impossible but the task would fall on me to lead the remaining people out of the darkness to come and into the light I thought me is this possible then I realized that the whole of the tribe was bowing to me hopeful I would be able to save them all from the pending doom the elders removed the cape of the previous prophecy the thing that got to me is it was Grey hounds old cape I asked them if it was true that he was the legend that stopped the beasts last time and they all nodded I felt so much power and so much pain at the same time I didn't realize how much it must have hurt Grey hound to see another prophecy walking side by side with him now I understand why he didn't like all the newer people in the tribe and why he had given me the hard shoulder I felt so guilty for not figuring it out all of a sudden we heard claps of thunder this is where it begins I suppose the beginning of the end of the world or the creating of the new one

Chapter 7: THE END OF WARS

within days the demons had attacked all towns and cities and people had fleas to the Forrest seeking refuge we could have killed them easy but they wanted to join our fight and save themselves we could fight better with our hands they fight better with their guns and so we let them into the fortress and allowed them to join up with us they had fled with the white flag the elders had warned me that my choices would have consequences if I refused the humans they would have been killed and on the full moon we would have lost all our power or so we thought the humans where more useful than we thought originally and yes I no I was human once but a lot has changed from then apparently the demons had spread across their lands tearing away at owns cities they lost their war against them by trying to kill everything I told hem that solution wouldn't work because people may still be trapped in their areas every now and then I would send a pack of wolves to find food and supplies for the humans see we wolves have our supplies right on our doorsteps we grew our own food and meat we can eat anything demons are good to eat gives us power but also gives us all we need but its not right to keep eating them for all we no they might want us to do that making us consume so much of them that we our selves become them Elise and me don't care what the elders think because human kind has brought married with them to the fortress however I would rather have their permission to marry a beautiful girl obviously we can not have children because we are not human or full wolves so it would be impossible however nothing can stop us trying or is that to rude anyway I figured if we where going to fight along side the humans they need to be taught how to fight like us as we are stronger faster and we never give in even when the odds are against us it takes ages and as soon as we train them they seem to start to give up as soon as a battle looks like it is lost they run away we never run even when it looks like we would die otherwise but we have honor and self respect so when they run or pull back with out our command we force them back into line as I said we are fast and stronger who would you rather die as a cowed or as a hero we tell them it makes them make up their minds very fast if they carry on running we kill them and say they got killed in the fight and that their bodies where lost in the fight and that then we give them an honorable send off even though we no the truth eventually we have soldiers out of them and my god I am so proud to be the reason they are who they are they are now fit to call themselves holy warriors of god we wolves have forged them new weapons stronger lighter weapons they tried to offer us guns but we cannot except them we tell them that they will need them for the fight to come Elisa and me are so in love we are married now after all the training was complete we had a human priest with wolves watching some humans don't think we deserve the right to be married but we reply to that with you came to us seeking safety shelter and weapons and tell us we do not have the right to marry all goes silent then no rumors no resistance is met even if their was we would just push them out into the woods see how long they last before they get killed and so we have created an army of last standers everybody has now got at least three jobs to be doing somehow people keep showing up and the fortress just seems to be filling up we are running short of room so we ask the humans if they will create houses for themselves just outside the fortress so that can free up our space and they then can be in control of their rules with guild lines from us of course they are not to go out on the full moon and also not to try to attack us we clear an area of Forrest and they set about creating a fortress of their own withing 2-3 weeks they had completed their wall and started on building their homes its amazing what demons can cause man to create it make us stronger but it made them faster to build and to create help for them its been a unlivable few months for me and Elisa the rest of the wolves want to go out and find other people and food so I guess I wanted that too but a couple of weeks ago an accident happened and Elisa was wounded and so shes now not allowed out of the fortress until she heals and believe me when I say I tore the demon to tinny pieces for doing what it did to her so shes grumpy but old Anthony is taking care of her she hates it but loves it it brings her back to the days before she was a wolf and it reminds us we are still part human as I leave our house I say to her Elisa you no I love you with all my heart in return she throws a pillow at me and says I love you too I turn as she says that and the pillow hits me in the face I say to her when I come home we shall continue this pillow fight even though we are all in imminent danger my focus is a pillow fight stupid right anyway its my turn to go out and look for food tonight so iv got one place planned out its somewhere iv wanted to go ever since I became a wolf

HOME

Chapter 8:HOME COMING PRESENT

I asked for a small platoon of soldiers to come with me and they came without a fuss so we set off for the town I used to live in I recognized on of the soldiers he was an elite it figures as he survived the first wave of demons I looked at his scares and then looked at mine and I punched him in the arm and laughed almost broke his arm by accident he laughed and waved it off I can tell im going to like this one I ask them what weapons they carry as I no the town I can use them strategically one said I am a sniper ill go up high or down low sire I asked the rest they all respond we are all trained to do what needs be done we have all said our goodbyes so well Elisa knows im coming back just in what state I will return we all walk out of the fortress I turn wolf and taunt the humans keep up if u can I stroll which to then is a running pace but they keep it if they live to the end of the day I might keep them as my personal guards chances are they wouldn't last though

it took us five hours to get to the town I looked in and just saw total mess and havoc I pointed out the church tower to the sniper he climbed to the top of the spire without a problem our training is working with them he checks and points that there is some people moving in I rush to see if I knew any of them I looked strait into the eyes of my mother I turned human and she froze then said you shouldn't have come home all of a suddenly she got dragged away from us just like Grey hound I collapsed to the floor the soldiers already in full throttle battle I sank deeper than I ever had all I could see was rage and anger I stood up turned wolf and killed all the demons that where killing my mum infrount of me the veteran that id punched earlier was literally jumping onto of the demon dogs and shooting them in the head iv never seen such commitment from a man before to kill one of these things I join in and feast making me more powerful I rip the remaining demons apart when I stand I see that was just the first horde the men where already tired so I tried to pull them back the sniper gave us the cover we required but he got caught in the middle he screamed at me to leave him and to worry about the rest I gave him the last of the vodka that id found he drank it and stood up pulled out his combat knife I ran with the others I all of a sudden herd him scream as they buchured him we will honnor him later I say to the soldiers we luckily had enough food for the winter in what we found I wonder how the other group got on but no time now to think and doubt what they where thinking about I was still feeling dark I told the soldiers to run as fast as they could and that id cover them until they where safe the veteran new what I was doing but he had no way to stop me was more powerful much bigger and much faster than him so he followed his men before he disappeared I spoke to him and said if we make it back to the fortress speak to me when you get their I need to ask you something he responded yes sire

with that he disappeared I stood my ground I pushed the demons back all of a sudden a massive flash came over my shoulder and I saw the veteran had stayed he knew what I was doing and wanted in he dropped his case of bulites and started to fire his M16 into the oncoming horde we killed about 200 demons before they pulled back to regroup I picked him up put him on my back and said hold on tight or you will fall off within seconds we where with the rest of the platoon within about 2 hours they where all home safe Elisa was waiting for me she saw my distress but didn't ask me anything the veteran came to me and said you requested me sire I responded yes you did well today id like to offer you a promotion you will stay by my side for the rest of this conquest until you die or we win do you except he looked at me and said you really don't need to ask me that you need to say how many demons do you need to kill before redemption I laughed

Chapter 9: HEAR COMES THE FLOOD

all the humans now had a basic knowledge of how to fight the demons encase the fortress was to become under attack because we needed to be able to defend our selves people have started to show real potential for things like magic I no that sounds so childish but they are creating fire and water from thin air and they are also creating buildings from the ground below them now even me as a human didn't have that ability they are becoming druids and yet they don't realize how powerful they are and so we are keeping quit because they could possible kill us with the demons mind you I don't think they would ever be that bad because we sheltered them either way they are starting to use their abilities against the demons hell what kills em makes it one less for us to worry about and so the hunt begins we must capture one keep it alive and torchure it till it learns to speak our language or it dies either way we will beat these things must have a weakness where did they come from vi no that sounds daft demons come from hell but I wanna be sure these are demons and I wanna be careful to not make a new ally with them and just as I thought things couldn't get weirder than they already have we now have blood suckers trying to kill our humans one night a couple of wolves where found dead this made Elisa very uneasy as if we didn't have enough to worry about so one night me and 4 wolves stood guard they new they where near their leader so they made them selves feel no fear even though we where all very scared we never could see them coming and yet tonight I was on the prowl nothing gets in without my permission and nothing leaves unless it is dead or dieing that may sound really sinister or really loyal but these are my people I am their Savior if this is going to be true then why are they not coming after me surely if they where then they would have won the war if they kill me then they win but tonight we have a weapon that hasn't been used before we are using bate I no its wrong but we used a child a wolf child not a human child that would just be a slaughter house and yes we have started to turn a few people with no chances otherwise of survival our blood can cure all disease and infection only problem is the feeding anyway we see something flying in the air it drops at such a speed that I jump onto its back I bite off its wings and force it to the ground it throws me off it but it is unable to fly away now so it tries to run it already is covered in blood the other 4 wolves cover the excites I stand and say you have nowhere to run and nowhere to hide and with that I knock it unconscious when it comes round I have gathered the elders and all of the council as well as the human leaders with my trust personal guard stood by my side with a gun aimed at this things head I ask the council for guidance on what these things where the oldest stood and said behold the vampires I looked at him in disbelief but I guess im standing hear and im not exactly human so I have no room to talk the elder walked up to it inspecting it and then said these vampires always where a trouble all hell has been realized god knows what els has been and with that the elder cut the head of the vampire off and started to explain the story of the vampires

vampires history

the vampires are lead by a man called count Draco an old name he has many names to this day including count Dracula the midnight biters and as most no them the princess of darkness

many years ago count Draco was working in his laboratory with his servants when the towns people found out he was actually working on something so terrible they wanted to stop him and so they forced him out of the laboratory and into the streets where they threw stones and sharp objects at him his wife and children where killed infrount of him and then they ended his life as he descended to hell he wasn't screaming like the rest and so the devil asked him if he wanted to escape hell and take vengeance upon the town that did this to him and his family in his rage he said yes and so the devil took a signature off count Draco he signed and was taken by death back to his body when he awoke he smashed his way out of the coffin and started to killed all the people as he finished the last one of the towns people the devil rose up and put a curse on the count saying you killed innocent people tonight the deal was for the people who killed you and so from now on you must drink blood every time it comes you will live forever and with that the devil was gone the vampire thought long and hard and he traveled the world alone an forever until he realized if he bites people and didn't kill them they would turn into his kind as well then the devil rose up and told him now that you are a race of people you must come with me so that I can protect you and with that the devil took the count but left all of his children of the night to wait for their leader to return when god herd of this evil creation he created a similar race to counter the actions of the devil and help his other creations live and with this came the werewolves one of the more powerful races known the vampires would be destroyed by them and then peace would be restored but like the vampires the wolves where cursed to only be able to use their power during the full moon and with that the wolves howl at the full moon even though over the centuries the wolves and vampires have fought they are the destroyers of them selves evil and good within them turns them into the monsters they are but one day a leader will descend from heaven to lead the wolves to destroy the vampire count however both wolves and vampires are rare to this day after the war of mankind striking both of them down forcing the wolves into hiding and the vampires where thought to be extinct until a warrior of god arrived on the planet he spoke of a prophecy that one day darkness would fall and when that day fell the vampires would rise up and destroy all that stood before them but that their was hope and that he would return in the form of a human and be changed to a wolf to fight the demons and the vampires

this day is the day when the wolves and humans stand side by side and humans where realizing they where not alone in this world and forces way above and out of their control are at work

Chapter 10: FORGING A NEW WEPON

well us wolves have found that the vampires cannot stand sunlight and also are weak like us against silver and so we have asked the humans to start to mine for silver nearby and make silver bullets so that they can take down our evil brothers in the sky aka the vampires we figured seen as god sent wolves and that god created us for the reason of beating the vampires well we think that god created us but then god left earth to create a new species to forget about us and that we where corrupt

every night I wake up screaming after having the nightmare about my mum being dragged away and killed in front of me it tears me apart but for the people I act normal but the wolves can tell im stressed and so Elisa asks me what is bothering me I ask her to sit down with me as my wife she would understand as soon as I tell her she feels guilty for not noticing it when I arrived back from my home town I mean it was quit bad but ill live I must live for the sake of both wolf and man kind she walks over to me pushes me onto the bed and starts to kiss me it makes me forget about the dream and more about something els before long the lights go out and you get the rest

….

next morning

no nightmares last night I wonder maby that is what helps us forget who and what we are even though I no Elisa is a cheeky girl but she knows how to please her husband anyway back to the war every man know he needs love and he needs respect I have that with my wife so I fight every day now to see my one true love see all that was human within me iv changed so much become a warrior I feel this darkness within me that I felt when my mum was killed that horrible feeling it was gone for now at least that's what mattered the most I felt the best I could at the moment and when the time came I would morn my loss unless I was killed first I mean am I really the chosen one I am a young adult but they seem so sure I will lead them to victory or to their deaths its kinda a hell of a lot of pressure even still I no what I must do I must first kill all remaining vampires then I must find a way to stop these demons the only problem is that we cannot track these vampires as they move among our people by night and by day are hidden its so hard to find them a few days ago I found one of my men hiding in the back of the barracks he was scared of the light I had to kill him to make an example of them even tho he was a good fighter the night before he was bitten I could tell I could smell his blood but I used to track the monster that did this to him and when I found it believe me it was begging to be killed I did after torturing it for hours and hours making it think I was going to finish it and finally I did after I got some information out of it telling it to tell me where the rest of its kind where and that's what hit me the hardest they where at my old house why was everything that was happening based around me and that bloody town I mean first the wolves then the demons now the vampires whats next zombies no now that will not happen I wont let it happen and besides we don't bury our dead we burn them just encase we asked the humans to do the same as we wouldn't want anything to be able to be used against us thus no zombies however the demons are doing something weird sometimes they take peoples bodies with them and put parts onto themselves its weird its like they are trying to provoke us into going into open combat with them because it would be like fighting against ourselves luckily they haven't found any parts of wolf anyway yer so the vampires they are in my home town so I thought I no what better chance to wipe them out when we get attacked by the demons and so I push through the lines after we finish off the wave I feast and think well to be fair im at full strength I run off and head to the town a few other wolves sense a feast is in order and some serious killing and so they follow their leader to the end of the Forrest and into the town that is now ashed except one house I run at the house and burst through the front door to find my mum sitting in the shadows I looked round the room how was she still alive I saw her die I swear I did and then it hit me I saw them dragging her away and yes they bite her a lot but who's to say that wasn't to mess with my head this has been a blow to me and by the time I realize what is happening the door slams behind me im in complete darkness and surrounded by vampires luckily I find out they are all hurt and my wolves are to close behind me they fight their way to me we all stand and say as a joke in the name of the lord we shall end you and tear the house down I see my mother crying but shes undead I have no feelings this woman made me hurt now its my time to hurt and fight back I make the wolves finish off the last of their pack while I deal with my mum I make it a quick death for her I figured that was a much better way to do it she gave birth to me yer she was a creature of the night but at least give her the respect that she deserved and the dignity anyway now that we killed most of the vampires we returned to the fortress and returned to the battle no one had died since I left so it was all OK Elisa pulled me into the house and asked me where I went I explained everything and finally was overcome by emotions and so she recalled my personal guard as well as the veteran to protect me at all costs while she joined the fight for the first time I let her loose on the battlefield and my god I thought the wolves where scary she is one hell of a fighter I watch her from the house and when she comes home she just starts to cook as if nothing had just happened I am amazed so much that I ask her where she learn that she said you always where watching my ass weren't you when we where training I nod and smile she sakes her ass and goes where you watching the movement of my hands then or the movement of my ass I wasn't going to lie she would be able to tell she smiled and wiped the blood off her hands and face we run upstairs and start to kiss each other as you get the drift of what happens no …..

next day (yes this is happening)

well last night there was a heavy explosion in the human fortress it was a gas leak and so us wolves sprung into action stopping it nobody was killed thank the lord anyway today we saw flashes of light on the mountain so me and the rest of the wolf pack went to the mountains we ran to where this all began from the humans decided to stay and guard the fortress we let them have their moment but I leave a few wolves close by just encase because im not bringing Elisa with me I love her but would rather she survived and so she remained their as we marched up the hill an horde of demons flew at us I just grabbed their jaws and cut them off then threw their corpses to the ground as did all the other wolves we pushed for the top of the mountain where the smoke came from I tell you we did one hell of a job on the demons we where moving at a faster pace than ever before I can even explain what drove us deeper into the mountain it was like we where being called in by something as we reached the top I looked back their was another horde waiting and advancing my wolves where tired they started to run at us but where deflected by some sort of shield I turned around and saw about 20 druids holding out their hands and muttering words another one came out from behind them and said come with us if you wish to be spared as they did the wolves and my self followed like sheep we didn't no where we where going or what would happen I ran up to the leader of theirs and asked how they lived after the first assault and he replied all will be revealed in time I was determined to find out how they lived I mean we came up the mountain that day and EVERYTHING was destroyed he eventually gave in and said as soon as the village was attacked we all woke up hear we where saved by the master after we gave up hope he didn't he was the one who saved you before and he saved all of you so far I was so confused but from then on I went silent I new id be told what I needed to no eventually and when I found out that we where just weapons of another force I was amazed

Chapter 11: THE ANGELS DESCEND

as we where descending to the druids new home we saw people happy and content how could they be when the world outside was tearing its self apart the world was literally being destroyed and they where playing mindless games when they saw me they stood and bowed to me as if I was in charge of them we moved into an open roofed room and he said this is where our messenger comes from

I stand and laugh at him he then asks me what im laughing at and with that a flash of blinding light hit the floor my instincts kick in and tell me to defend my self but what I am amazed to see is that in my wolf form I was bowing to this light and that the wolves behind me where bowing further than me he fell and folded up his arms in all his glory I felt unable to keep my eyes off him he was flying so I said are you and before I finished he said I am no demon far from it I am one of the angels your father sent brothers the angels want to free you of your curse but we need you to do one thing for us leave the demons to us I look at him and say I feel like I no you he said brother it is me its Michael I look so confused he then says the prophecy we gave human kind that an angel would fall change into a wolf and save the human race the wolf race and druids

and you are I said

he responded an angel of the lord hear to protect the human race I then laughed and said an angel he says yes I say to him so if angels are real why haven't you come quicker the angel keeping calm says do you honestly think you are the only species god created we have spread out across the galaxy to protect all forms of life from these demons its a hard world heaven needs humans though you are the only ones now that can restore peace Anthony it is your destiny weather u except it or not to protect these people after this who knows where you will go or what you will become I look at the angel with disparaging what about Elisa and the rest of my people he the angel responded they will be saved if you will sacrifice

I didn't realize how serious this was .....

Chapter 12: TIME MUST COME AND MAN MUST SURVIVE

well time has come to make my mind up but its not a difficult decision to make I mean my life for the rest of the planet well the angel never said I died I just needed to sacrifice never said what needed to be sacrificed but whatever it takes ill destroy all these demons and free my people as well as the humans and so the angel flies me back to the fortress and is greeted by the council both human and wolf

the angel bows as does everyone els and then flies off

the council has a lot to ask me but none of it about what the angel said they thought it was a sign from the heavens that people are watching us and making me aware that a lot of people are watching and waiting for the sign all of a sudden I come up with a plan I will make a new clan of wolves and humans alike they will be called the blood biters and once this war is over if we win they will kill all evil things and wait for the next coming because this isn't the last time this will happen

as the leader of the packs the council has given over the Armour of the last warrior to make this commitment and the weapons he was allowed to use including a sword I looked at them they said times change this time they are stronger than before and we are stronger too so the Armour was smelted by the druids put together by the humans and the wolves made sure it had our crest emblem on it and then Elisa made her own personal guarding part on it she put a heart emblem on it and said when you go into battle know that the clan and the people are behind you and our love will protect you

I look back at the clam and say my people I will restore peace and harmony just as I am about to leave Elisa asks to speak to me she says im pregnant I am so proud but at the same time if I didn't give it up people would die and I wont let that happen I look at her and smile and say im so happy and proud to be a father I shall return when the land is safe and with that me and the blood biters leave the fortress possibly for the last time but who knows maby one day I will return I just keep my thoughts on the battle all the men and wolves are Armored up I guess you could say the world ha fallen into darkness an I would return it to the light this must stop where it all started up in the mountainside and then down in the remains of the town I grew up in this is going to be one hell of a battle we must battle horde after horde and hope that the devil himself pulls his troops back and then I must seal the gate to hell with my sacrifice the angels have started the fight we join in they look at us and bow we bow back then strait into open air combat it was hours before the base of the mountainside was under our control now to fight the Forrest now this bit was tricky because the Forrest was so ark the angels just threw lights into the Forrest the demons seemed to be getting more and more aggressive so we know we are getting close all of a sudden the flames consume an area all the angels say this is where u must choose and they fly off leaving the blood biters in the darkness except the chaos and flames all the humans are firing all they have got the wolves are slashing and cutting away at it then it all blows up on the floor next to us all pushes us back and all the demons are dragged back into hell but something bigger comes free it is just made of flames I remember what the angels say I see it heading for all the humans and wolves it call out to it and jump at the flames it grabs hold of me for a while I feel nothing and then I feel pinned to the floor by a spike through my shoulder it pierces the Armour and forces me to the floor and a voice comes to me time has frozen the wolves and the men have frozen I hear a voice that booms like thunder saying you must choose a life of sorrow alone on this planet but you get to save it or go to Ur doom everyone els lives their will be no escape this time ANTHONY and with that I stand up I take my final bow and say let them people go this is my destiny I killed your vampires I killed your servants so now its only fare that you kill me this stuns the demonic voice and it says but you will willing give up your life knowing that these people didn't care about you I respond to the voice I don't need to no they care because I love them all the same they would die for me and I will die for them and with that the voice says so be it the planet is restored people around the world celebrate but I am dragged to hell for what seems an eternity but I smile all the same I know that my baby my wife and my people are safe all of a sudden a light shines down onto me an angel came for me I thought they forgot I was their and it carries me to heaven where a man wherein a white jacket is waiting for me he says you have one wish Anthony what is that wish I say to go home to my wife and my child and with that the man said I am the highest power hear and with that everything went dark ……

Chapter 13:HOME COMING

three months had passed since the war was over the clean up had began and the clan was dispersing for some bizarre reason they all thought I was dead when in a bean of light my body was dropped infrount of the council they all started to cry and sob thinking I was dead when I started to moan they then started to cheer I was greeted with much appreciation my amour was still in tact except the shoulder pad was destroyed I gave that to the council and spoke up to the people with my blood biters behind me I said you are all free of demons for now but they will return one day when man kind is weak we must rebuild but prepare for the next assault it could be tomorrow it could be a thousand years but it will happen we must learn to love and that within each and everyone of us there is an evil we must learn to find another way to vent instead of summoning I was in heaven and in hell at the same time the devil is real we must be ready for his rising and with that I turned round picked Elisa up the council asked where will you go I say that's not for anyone els to know I will appear when the world turns to darkness and will be resurrected when it is time you will see the signs and with that I carried Elisa off and into the distance and lived happily ever after

the end
or is it

moral lesson in life
witb the morals meaning that everyone has evil inside them but nothing that out ways good no matter who you are you deserve a chance to live and express yourself thank you so much for being hear with me along this emotional roller coaster

with special thanks to the following:

Sarah d

Steve b

Elisa g

Diana n

my family

my fans

its been a long two years and its ready to end now so thank you so much ill be writing again soon
love
Ross Anthony Chandler

blood biters children of war

Chapter 1 first sight

The last thing i remember their was a massive explosion then i felt warmth against my body The next thing i no im back at the wolves castle Elisa looking at me with a big bump on her belly The first instinct should be that werewolves can not have children but she looks troubled Thinking back to what had just happened i start to think what if its a demon behind me I start to put my guard up when all of a sudden it hits me she's looking right at me as im walking towards her She screams at me to stop and a lot of human soldiers put up a wall infrount of her i stand still Feeling like an outcast then one of the elders comes forward and askes me to recall all i remember I feel devastated that they don't trust me but i answer the question the wall disperses and she runs towards me Arms wide to hug me i feel confused but i carry on as i had been walking for what felt like a lifetime Apparently it had been months since me and the unit had left to fight with the angels and had heard no news of Me so assumed i was dead apparently mimics of me had come, demon illusions as the last of their Power was leaving the planet but they hadn't seen me since the war ended apparently humans are a lot More cautious of us now than during the war

Chapter 2 the returning hero

While everyone else was saying i was a hero in my mind i was more worried about Elisa as she was carrying a baby Yet no one else seemed bothered by this i had been taught that no werewolf could ever concede a baby as they Are part human part wolf so it would never work but apparently they have done all the checks in the history and Said that their is no proof of such things however its tickling my mind the more i think about it the more it worries Me and so i go to the elders who will not answer me only question me on why i am asking them these things Elisa can see im worried and so she tries to comfort me but i can remember my trainer telling me about what Could happen if a baby wolf was born and why it was against the rules but the people keep saying that im their hero And the humans start to move back into the old towns and cities as they re build their lives we stand guard just encase any stranded demons have been left behind once they confirm they are settled and can defend themselves we back off back into the woods now that our job is done we can now both morn our dead hero's

Chapter 3 birth of the first Reaper

All of a sudden i woke up hearing Elisa screaming my name instinct kicked in again but this time it was fear of loosing Her when she told me her waters had broken i was in shock i didn't no what to do as this wasn't a normal birth She was in her human form so the baby would be born easier as this is the first wolf human combo we ran to the elders Who told us they had known a ritual in one of the scrolls that the humans had brought as a gift in a time of peace And it had revealed that a wolf and a human had become the perfect monster or the greatest savoir and so it must be raised in a peaceful place luckily since the war was over this was the safest place for a baby to grow up but it only had been 6 months since she found out she was pregnant so i was overwhelmed with shock we got her sedated put her in a birthing pool and after two hours a baby was born hairy but a baby none the less the elders blessed the baby but under the new laws that where past on werewolves we had to leave the safety of the castle till the baby became a boy aged fourteen to test his skills so me and Elisa set out on our own adventure but before we left we had to name our little monster for many years i had been thinking i was dead so i suggested a strong name would be white angel Elisa didn't agree and so as a joke i said lets just call him reaper as i said it Elisa agreed and so little reaper was named and we set off to the Forrest to set up a new home for us

Chapter 4 finding a new world

Once we had cleared the castle and couldn't find any human settlements for a long way we realized we where safe from anyone finding us that new us and as long as we could keep ourselves to ourselves and the baby safe that's all that mattered to us and so i started the construction of a shelter for us like the first shelter i tried to get to when i was turned to a wolf only i cleared a path set up a nice fireplace it only took me a few hours to nock together if i do say so myself it was a work of art Elisa saw my look of achievement and lent on me and stupidly made a joke saying its good but its not quiet carling i instantly burst out into a fit of laughter id already started to make the cot for the baby when i out of the corner of my eye saw a figure all dressed in black but Elisa was one step ahead of me i broke into my wolven form as a warning but by the time id changed he was gone i couldn't even sense him their it gave Elisa the creeps but i let it slide over my head thinking it was our imagination playing tricks on us but over the next few days things started getting stranger and me and Elisa would start to get annoyed at each other thinking that the other was playing tricks but what was being found was warnings that they wanted the baby so while i was awake i would guard the house then Elisa would take over the next morning we found a warning saying you have two days either we take the baby or you give us the baby this made me agitated i thought maybe the humans had found out we had left the safety of the castle and sought us out for revenge for their fallen comrades but this was the final strew i saw a figure and i decided to chase it as i was far superior at running but my god this guy had speed on his side i finally caught up with him grabbed hold of the hood as it was still moving but it was empty i realized it was a trap to draw me away horrified i ran back to the house to find it empty Elisa and the baby nowhere to be found i tried to sense or even pick up a trail but it just wasn't their it didn't make sense and no i had lost the one thing that could tip the balance again i noticed a note on the floor it read we warned you now its to late i needed some serious help and so i ran back to the castle to find a bloodbath had happened while we had been gone

Chapter 5 the city of blood and bones

As i was running through the city all i was seeing was dead wolves but no sign of struggle or anything but their was holes ripped in their chests and hearts where all over the floor what strikes me as weird is the fact that they are all next to the right bodies and all the bones are by their sides Asif to say they had been pulled out of their bodies i rushed through this city now destroyed by chaos but no signs of struggles i ran to the elders one was still alive barely as i walked in he said demon why have you come to taunt me in my dying hour i replied im no demon im just a lonely wolf in need of help finding a lost wife and a son he then said my god its the real chosen one ur mimics have been back again i said i need to no some information about this hood i sat him up he was coughing blood really badly he wasn't going to make it much longer he looked at the hood then at me then at the hood he then spoke saying you may have won the battle with the demons but the war is just beginning i reminded him about the battle he said the angels where hear to protect us until you where ready and now you are ready they have left us he then told me the cult of castell diablo has taken ur son to raise hell ur wife will be sacrificed and ur son he then drew his last breath and past i needed to find where this cult could be found and if their where any other survives of the massacre even all the young wolves where dead almost perfect cuts in the chests that worried me and the fact that my wife was going to be the start of the new war i had to find at least one survivor as i was alone but i didn't feel it i felt the presence of the angels again all of a sudden the blinding light landed infrount of me i shied away from it as usual the angel tried to speak it was Michael he saw all the bodies and decided to burry them all in a second he then looked at me and asked where the child was i was still in shock so i couldn't speak he then shouted at me to show him the baby when i regained control of myself i explained that he had been taken he then swore and vanished in my head i laughed to myself i thought god if you can hear me one of your angels just swore he broke the rules as i said that Michael reappeared i heard that you shouldn't mock me if you new how serious this was you would no not to make a joke of it i asked him what is going on i thought we won the war he replied no if you had listened to me it was a small battle in the midst of all of the war remember their are other worlds we have to protect to instinct kicked in i said screw the other worlds im worried about this world alone he then replied and that's why you don't have many angels on hand to help you every world we loose the devil gets stronger you may have just lost this world because of your stupidity do you know who took ur baby i replied with castell diablo the angel kicked his feet Asif to say i feel like iv been so stupid for asking i respond didn't you no about their movement he was trying to play it cool but failed to do so they are a clan devoted to chaos and destruction their god is the devil himself and he's offered a reward for your son and wife no wonder they came hear first my reaction was rage how could you do this to me how could you let someone good get hurt you should of told me before you weren't ready Michael replied now that we no we can trust you the whole reason i came for the baby was to protect him the almighty has order the protection of your son as the highest priority then i responded secondly why didn't you protect him when you new he was born well i tried to but i couldn't do much as castell diablo is a demon cult Michael said with senseor remorse i decided to let him explain what was going to happen if they got the baby and my wife it was a gruesome tale about how the devil would raise an army to destroy what is left of humanity and the planet once he had finished he asked if any wolves had survived i looked around to see if any others had we looked for an hour to no avail and so i left the castle and fort of the dead and dammed with Michael

Chapter 6 new blood new army

For what came next i am not proud of in a rage i ran into the nearest city to the Forrest and found a random person as Michael was trying to calm me down knowing that my wife and son where going to cause so much evil if i didn't have an army to stop this cult i ran strait into the human government chamber and demanded to be seen by the humans if they had any respect of the resent war they would respond as they all gathered Michael and me began to explain what will happen as we are just short of finishing a human called Norman stepped forward and spoke i think you will find we have lost enough people for a lifetime this is not our battle so why should we believe you i snapped i didn't have time for this petty human so i bit him enough to turn him he went into spasms i replied because i need a dam army to keep your world safe from the likes of your own kind if we don't stop them they will come hear next i am the last werewolf my wife my son are gone i have nothing to loose Michael then spoke up and said angels cannot fight your battles anymore this planet is lost to us i am hear as it was my responsibility to deliver this message if you don't fight then why should we i then walked out and started randomly biting people not enough to kill but enough to turn people as their soldiers looked nervous in the square i spoke and said their is a war coming the demons will be back the castle for the wolves has fallen i am all that remains remember the wolves protected you when you had no where else to go now the last wolf is on ur doorstep asking i need strong men to volunteer to help me take down a cult of magical beings i cannot do it alone all the people i have bitten already will be under my control and i will lead them merciless to their deaths you have left me no choice but if you give me soldiers to fight this coming war i will help you win the war i was chosen to fight this battle and i cannot see any easy way to do this as i said this a explosion happened i heard the sound of dying people i look at the crowed and say i will save you today but who is hear when all the wolves are gone as quickly as i had said that i had arrived on the battlefield of the dead

Chapter 7: true honour among dead brothers

When i arrived on the battlefield i realized what i was up against this was far worse than demons or vampires this was our fallen wolves i saw brothers and sister destroying humans it was devastating seeing zombie wolves but then as i stretched my muscles my new found brothers landed by my side the people i had turned had already taken their places next to me a few minuets later soldiers stood just behind us and we pushed forwards i started to make heist towards the strongest zombie wolf smashed him to pieces but it didn't finish him it takes a silver bulite to kill a wolf so another wolf could not finish them humans loaded their guns i ordered them to stand down till we had got them to a state they couldn't hurt any humans but like wise no new blood wolves would be hurt for some reason they all did amazing for their first time in combat a couple of the younger ones fell prey to the zombies but in every war it is impossible to not loose any soldiers so i kept pushing forward once the battle was over humans swept the zombies down after i returned with the five wolves to the square and Michael had already made a outpost for people to volunteer to become a wolf when we arrived back i turned into my human self to show how we can be normal shaped just like them and to also teach the new blood how to change back i felt truly hurt that i had just had to kill my brothers even though they where already dead as i walk out i see a line back to the other side of the square Michael your relived go back to your commander get more angels we need as many as we can get as i said that he disappeared and people looked to me to lead them to their future

Chapter 8: no mercy in sight

Im back at the house Elisa seems to be crying but not with sadness with happiness then she sees me and her expression darkens Asif she had seen a ghost i step towards her she screams and runs away but she cant she starts to get back up but she is flipped over by an unseen force and raised into the air im watching all this then i see the hooded men going into the house and retrieving our baby reaper i try to scream i cant do anything i try to hit them and help Elisa but she is frozen and now bleeding out of her arms and legs but she's still alive then the hooded man looks me right in the face and says this is what is happening to your wife ur child is ours now i wake screaming so loud all of the city is woken by me another bad dream this is the seventh night in a row this has happened i just shrug it off as i have done all the other morning im going to get my fucking wife back and my son i will save the day i work up a sweat when i go for my morning run as a human so they don't get to scared of me they know who i am as my tattoos are recognized i got them the first day i arrived and it meant that all the wolves could be tracked by me and the government so they couldn't hide or run away during training even though they allowed me to stay they where not happy however i was training their armies to prepare them for combat that i had no idea how serious it could be or how strong the cult is as the days training finishes a flash hits all the other wolves and humans Evert their eyes me i put a hand out and shake the angels hand he's brought more to help me train the new blood army seen as wolves are gods creation to protect humans all the wolves bow to the angels almost out of respect the real warriors of the universe the angels bow back as the wolves are the creation of their father too the angels stick by my side and wont talk to humans to much as they know that humans are not as creative and as helpful in the up coming battle after a few weeks all twenty angels have trained two hundred wolves and four thousand soldiers to fight with them Michael comes and sits with me while i eat and asks the worst question possible are your dreams showing you where they are i reply how do you no about my dreams he says because the cult knows we are hear they don't no what we are doing but my father has told me hell has her eyes on you i dodge the question by saying that the transformation to humans has been taught to the wolves he asks again tell me what you see in your dreams its in my house when i abandoned them they came for them i reply Michael looks confused how long where you gone for i said maybe a minute he then looked at me vanished and re appeared but he was injured another angel noticed and dragged him off and a bluer of light exploded from the tent a few seconds later the angel was back he told me a message from Michael your house they came from within your house their was a cave they dug underneath ur house and took your wife by surprise i look angrily at the floor thinking how stupid i was to think we where safe i thank the angel and he goes back to wherever the hell angels are from to check on micheal my fight is down hear not up their and so the recruitment drive has run dry so as promised once we had finished training we left the city it looked similar to the town i grew up in just a lot bigger we move off and head for death mountin to see if the druids will join us rather than sitting back and letting nature take its course its a three day treck and because we have humans with us we have to leave them at the bottom of the mountin because of the sacredness of the stones and of course we didnt want to upset the druids any futher than we already had by coming up unanounced however when we arived it was already to late they had their hearts ripped out of the chests just like the wolves had but this time in writting their was a haunting messege we warned you we where coming for all of your kind all the shrines had been destroyed and decemated i shed a tear but i new all the wolves could hear my thoughts so we charged back down the mountin to the soliders i new exactly where i was going and this was a one way trip i looked at the soliders and asked for any volateers after making a speech, i no this is going to be a one way ticket for anyone who comes with me but if you want to join me and the wolves and give whatever has been killing so point perfect then join me and help me put these fuckers back into the ground that they belong in, a rally cry no one moved all the soliders stepped forward and joined our ranks i turned their special forces into wolves their skills will be needed they had already signed their life to the cause once they where all wolf i looked up a full moon we ran so fast that the ground was barely touched by us within seconds we where outside my house that had the forrest burnt down all the guns where left outside the ring we waited till i saw a hooded figure step outside the house and i realized i may have been to late i saw little reaper coverd in blood but i didnt care he was my legacy he was the first wolf boy i had to protect him out of blood lust and the full moon i jumped out then the battle began

chapter 9: falling angels teares of fire

as i moved forwards their was a blast of light stronger than normal something large fell from the sky it was the angels on what looked like a titan it started fireing balls of flames one of the angels caught my eyes he winked of course it was micheal he had wings on this time asif just to scare his foe he started flying i used my last resort battle cry we charged in didnt wanna be left on the sideline for this battle as we joined the fight more species arived druids, humans, more wolves but their was an eruption on the ground beneth my feet i felt it rumbling i dived backwords all hell seemed to be coming out of the ground in the cornor i could see Elisa but she was smiling at me she wasnt afraid she knew her man was coming for her she was carrying baby reaper so i new he was safe so the angels changed from flames to acid dropping as much as they could down the hole to keep the demons suppressed i new we didnt have very long i jumped over the acide wolves following and druids supporting the angels in their titan humans held a perimeter to stop anything els leaving the feild i was gunning for the cult when all of a sudden i jumped into one of the hoods i felt like i couldnt move i hit the ground so hard with all the strenth in my body i couldnt Elisa saw my struggle and she screamed an explosion of energy burst into me i managed to stand barly all the other wolves where out for the count it was amazing i was still standing i could see elisa struggle then her eyes went wide i saw the silver knife rammed through her chest i was to late but maybe i could save Reaper the ground shook again i new what was coming was bad it was massive the titan couldnt hold the hole anymore demons flew out of the hole into the midst the humans where wiped out within a few swipes so i orderd the wolves to pull back and re enforce the perimiter to stop any streys from getting out one demon could wipe out a city as i did this i heard the voice that made shivers go down my spine he started the rituel with my wifes blood i wasnt letting this happen as i grabbed hold of his head he grabbed my arm and threw me into a tree two hundred meaters away not a problem i got up and ran back at him and his followers he wisperd your son is mine i thought over my dead body he replied my pleasure how could he hear my thoughts he looked at me with shock i realized who he was it was

chapter 10: beckys return

how hadnt i seen this coming when i asked her she said remember when you returned me to the edge of the forrest everyone blamed me for the deaths of their children i got ran out of town id of been better off dead because of you but then the cult picked me up asked me if i wanted to forfill my destiny to kill my savior and his family how could i refuse all the carnege that was going on around me i was to focused i begged her to let my son go and let me end this she smiled blood running down her cheek i dont think so the legend says i shall kill this baby and the world will fall to darkness like you left all of us in when you ran out of the camp to deffend ourselves from ur kind didnt you wonder why i only targeted places i new ud been to i followed the survivers of the first demon attack to find where your kind slept then waited and now how are all the wolves not these mongrules i mean even ur fucking wife is dead how does it feel to have absoluty everything you have ever known of love killed now i will finish what i started

sure enough she drew a silver sword out threw my baby to one of the other followers i was growling teeth glicening i heard micheal crash to the ground he could handle himself for now i had worse to deal with the bitch who killed my wife and held a sword to my son time for revenge she killed all my kind just to stabb at me

chapter 11: the death of true love

she was a lot faster than i remember her being she cut my arm without even breaking a sweat i was running round her so fast to creat a dust storm the battlle stopped everyone was watching us i didnt care if the whole world watched me tear this little bitches head off she could still see me as i ran strait at her she grabbed my neck and threw me into a tree then jumped into the air landed right next to me she missed me with the sword as she did it it was almost like she was taunting me she blew me a kiss she turned her back and started to walk away from me no way i was going to let her get the best of me i swipped for her neck she managed to predict where i was going to attack and put the silver sword in my pathway throwing me off balance micheal couldnt get involved no one else was alowed to come into this fight she drew up her hand tov jesture me to come to her i floated through the air luckily i played stupid just when i was within reach of her i smashed my claw into her rib cage she was stunned and in shock that she fell to the ground her followers looked as nerverous as her as i stood up i screamed you killed my brothers and sisters you killed my wife now im going to tear ur spine out of ur ass ran at her she was still in shock i smashed into her and smashed her head into the ground it exploded i stand and start to walk away i hear a giggle behind me next to the body their is now two of becky i swere and they both draw silver swords i fugred this could go on for a life time outside the circile i could see the wolves trying to break the barrier i orderd them to stand back and wait as im thinking that i feel extream emount of pain i look down and see the two swords through my chest the demons are loving seeing me in pain i collapse becky is behind me just one now she wispers in my ear now look as i kill your son michael was screaming coverd in acid all the other angels start to collapse my wolves are locked in hand to hand combat with the demons and the cultists she walks towords my son i creep up crawling on the ground behind her bleeding out but still fighting to keep myself alive for my son at least she raises him up another explosion another wave of angels lands the ground shakes so hard this is no angel this is something diffrent

chapter 11: decending gods and riseing demons

i couldnt believe my eyes he was just a pure white light in the darkest of places demons where running back down the hole asif they feared him he walks to the barrier and smashes it in one hit and walks through at the exact same time a demon exploades out of the ground sorry not a demon the devil now this is a titan battle all this because of my baby Reaper they lock into a battle they are massive me and becky are stood underneath them while becky is distracted i push my claw through her chest i hear her scream out and go limp in my arms the devil looks at me and summons fire around her i dont care my son is in their i jump over the fire grab my son and hold him in my arms i craddled him he was crying i wisperd dont be scared daddy and mummy are hear even not if in body in spirit my world goes dark after a while i come round the devil is pulling back into the ground and what looks like a god is standing victorious standing over me i no my time is drawing near he transforms into a human sized person he walks up to me in a really soft voice he asks if he can see my son i offer him up he wispers a few words in the ear of my son afterwoods he looks at me and asks me the question iv been waiting to hear he says if you have one wish what would it be my responce to make sure my son is protected from this world as i say that god respondeds well seen as you are one of my angels and so was elisa born as humans to stand in and protect them when the time came you would be put together by nature and have a son the true savior of this world i smile im fading i can feel my life force leaving me a woman walks up to me god says this is gemma she will protect your son she will raise him and tell him of your legend you will return with me to heven and be with your wife i hand the baby reluctantly to gemma i beg her to look after him as i draw my last breath i say i love you baby reaper......

chapter 12: home comming in heven

when i woke i could feel arms rapped arround me it was elisa she was smiling at me she had wings and so did i our skin was soft not rough like when we where wolves we where in the house we had built over the years i watched down on baby reaper i watched him grow into a boy but i was scared of the war that was to come i new he would have a tough time i wanted to be their with him but until the time when we are needed we angels remain in heven till the war really starts i was just a solider he is the hero that world needs

THE END

soon to return blood biters : the legend of the white Reaper

special thanks to

lady gemma bradshaw (my rock in this)

wife elisa (from start to end you will be hear)

demon slayer chandler (big bro i love you)

mother angel (mum you are amazing i love you)

saint micheal (for being hear for me rescently)

rapeie dan (cloraphorm boy)

mother tracy (enjoy my story)

Printed by Libri Plureos GmbH in Hamburg, Germany